Finding Hope in Seasons of Disappointment and Loss

An Interactive Prayer Journal Created for Women Battling with Miscarriage and Pregnancy Loss

ANGELICA GUNN

This Journal Belongs To

Name:

Date:

Names of Angels:

Printed in the USA by 48HrBooks (www.48HrBooks.com)

This journal is dedicated to my husband, Caleb; our three earthly babies, Aa'Kayla, Caleb Jr., Aubree; and our angels in heaven, Faith, Aiden, and Kaylei. Thank you for supporting me daily, believing in me, and inspiring me to share our story.

Table of Contents

Table of Contents continued

A Note from the Author

Hello, Beautiful! What a brave soul you are! I am truly grateful that you're here. This journal was created with true purpose and God's timing. My husband and I endured some of the toughest trials of our lives when faced with secondary infertility and recurrent miscarriages. It was a trying time and a true test of our faith, marriage, love, and commitment.

The pain behind it all led me to a really dark place. I lost friendships, I lost myself, I lost my true sense of purpose in these battles. I felt alone, angry, jealous, and tarnished. But none of those things I believed were true. The more difficult things became, the more I learned to rely on God for strength. I tried placing my hope in others for so long only to be let down by their lack of care, support, and love. God promises that he will never leave us nor forsake us.

Though you feel alone, though it's hard to see God in the midst of loss, God is there, waiting with open arms for you to surrender your brokenness to him. Thank you for allowing me to be a vessel in your journey as you seek peace, healing, and restoration.

Introduction

Thank you for purchasing this journal. This journal was created to provide a space for women to release the emotions, devastation, and heartache of miscarriage and pregnancy loss. Writing is therapeutic, and throughout our journey with secondary infertility and recurrent miscarriages, I used journaling as a way to express myself without feeling like I was being judged or unheard. The devastation that lies behind losing a baby is like no other, especially when you've battled with trying to become pregnant only to have your heart and womb emptied of the joy and excitement. My prayer is that as you read and interact with this journal, you find true peace, hope, and guidance. I hope that you find love and build a true relationship with God. God and my family are the only reasons I was able to find true healing. I pray that for you. I pray that you become surrounded by love, that you realize you are not alone, and that you find a way to love yourself again throughout this journey.

"The Lord is close to the brokenhearted and saves those who are crushed in spirit." Psalm 34:18

Before we get started, I would like for you to use this space to write down what you hope to get out of this journal. Remember, you can be as open and honest as you need to be: this is a safe space, a place where you can freely express the depths of your heart.

So do not fear, for I am
with you; do not be dismayed,
for I am your God. I will
strengthen you and help you;
I will uphold you with my
righteous right hand.

Isaiah 41:10

Miscarriage Is Devastating.

How Do I Cope?

My husband and I suffered our first miscarriage on May 11, 2015. It was Mother's Day and also my dad's birthday. We were absolutely devastated. Before going through our own miscarriages, I only had knowledge of one person in our family who has experienced the loss of a baby. I am sure that there are more who have experienced loss, but due to the lack of support, and fear of what others would think, they probably chose to not disclose their losses. We had two more miscarriages during our journey, and all of the losses left us empty.

So many women and men are dealing with miscarriage and pregnancy loss silently, and my mission and purpose is to change that. It is completely unhealthy to bottle up your grief and silence your heart's damaged wounds. You deserve to be heard, supported, and acknowledged.

I remember our miscarriages vividly, and I am sure that as I create this journal I will shed many tears as I relive some of the most painful moments of my life.

Throughout our journey, I used writing as a way to escape the harsh reality of our circumstances. It gave me permission to feel, to scream, to cry, to vent without judgement. It helped me release so many different emotions. I found myself often sitting in darkness, even when surrounded by light. I felt alone, even when I knew deep down that God and my husband were with me. The enemy lies to us often. He makes us believe that we are alone, that no one cares about us, that no one loves us, and that our circumstances define who we are and who we will become. All of that is untrue. We are fearfully and wonderfully made, we are loved, we are chosen, and even in seasons of loss, we are not alone. God sits right beside us with open arms.

"Cast all your anxiety on him because he cares for you."
1 Peter 5:7

How are you coping? Do you feel supported in your journey? Or do you feel alone?

Battling with the Emotions of Miscarriage/Pregnancy Loss

So many emotions occur when I think back on our journey. I often felt angry, sad, disappointed, broken, empty, and guilty. I blamed myself a lot. I felt everything was my fault even when it wasn't. I always asked myself what I could have done to save our babies, and felt that somehow something I did caused the miscarriages. I was jealous of pregnant women. I hated going out in public. I felt embarrassed. So many waves of emotions, so many days crying a river of tears, and so many moments of darkness. I battled with depression heavily after our first miscarriage, and it only got worse with the second and third. I was in a really dark place. Not many knew, but I was suicidal. I felt incomplete and robbed of my joy and peace. The truth is, my pain disabled me so much that I couldn't be me anymore. I couldn't be a wife, a mother to my daughter, a sister, or a friend. I couldn't be any of those things, because all of me was broken.

"Come to me, all who are weary and burdened, and I will give you rest." Matthew 11:28

How often have you felt broken? How often has the pain felt so debilitating that everything else in life stops moving and you only stand still in your grief?

How You Grieve May Not Be How Your Spouse/Partner Grieves

Our journey greatly affected our marriage. Most days I wanted to scream at my husband because I couldn't understand how he wasn't crying hysterically or showing any emotion. It drove me nuts. There I was, constantly in a puddle of my own tears, and he would just sit there quietly. It bothered me a lot because I assumed his lack of tears meant that he didn't care and wasn't affected by our losses. I often lashed out at him, and if I had known then what I know now, I can assure you our days would've been a lot easier back then. The truth of the matter is, people grieve differently, and we must respect our spouses and allow them to grieve in their own way.

When I take the time to truly put myself in my husband's shoes, I see our journey differently through his lens. I carried our babies, so I may be more emotionally attached than him due to that fact alone. My body experienced the trauma, not his. I went through changes physically and emotionally because of it, and though they are his babies too, he cannot fully understand it from my view, as he didn't physically experience the losses. I think that a lot of times I felt alone in that, just feeling like he couldn't fully grasp the depth of my pain. But I had to remind myself that it wasn't that he didn't want to understand or didn't try to, it was simply that he couldn't. We spent lots of time grieving on our own separately. We would open up and talk a little, but mostly our journey through grief consisted more of us walking alone through it than side by side. It wasn't that we wanted it to be this way, we just didn't know how to talk through our pain.

The truth of the matter is, miscarriage/pregnancy loss is hard, and grief is a journey that can never be explained. There is no road map or tour guide through it. The only way to persevere through grief is through God alone. He is our strength, our healer, our provider, and our redeemer. It is only through the lens of God that we can walk the path of grief and still be encouraged and uplifted through it. My husband reminded me of this constantly during our journey, and he helped me turn more to God in prayer rather than relying on myself to get me through the pain of our losses. God kept me, he showed up for me constantly, and without him, I wouldn't have developed the strength to keep fighting through the storms. Pain is temporary, but hurt can last forever if you don't release it and heal from it completely.

I created a list of suggestions to better help couples on their journey through grief:

-Never force your feelings onto one another.

-Give each other space and time to process what has happened.

-Listen before speaking and offering a response when your partner is opening up to you.

-Do things together to honor and remember your baby/babies.

-Remember that your way of grieving may not identify with your partner's way of grieving, and that is okay.

-Pray together.

-Read your Bibles.

-Ask if the other person needs or wants a hug or to be comforted.

-Meditate.

-Listen to music, write letters to your babies, and even write to one another if that is an easier way to express yourselves.

-Go for walks.

-Attend counseling, either together or separately.

-Watch a movie or do something that you both enjoy to free your mind.

-Love each other through it, and be patient with one another.

"Two are better than one, because they have a good return for their labor." Ecclesiastes 4:9

In what ways could you and your partner better your journey through miscarriage and grief? How can you better support one another through it?

Lost in Brokenness

The emptiness left behind after our miscarriages led me down a path of darkness. I often felt lost, hurt, and numb.

I found myself drowning in my own tears.

My heart was completely shattered, and most days I am still trying to put back together all of the pieces.

Brokenness is the state of being broken.

It is waking up knowing you have people counting on you but feeling so much heartache that it paralyzes you.

It is feeling so engulfed in grief that you can't eat, sleep, or drink.

It is losing all of your will to fight because you're weak from all of the tears and weight bearing down on your heart.

I felt powerless most days. I would wake up to the sun rising, with no joy for seeing its beauty. I would lie in bed all day with no desire to face the world outside our doors. Looking back on this season of my life,

I can tell you that brokenness tried to take me completely out.

I desired nothing more than to have and hold our babies in my arms, and each day that went by without them felt like the longest day ever.

I felt completely shattered. My womb cried out daily for our babies. My heart was so heavy that sharp pains would cloud my chest. My eyes were so red that blood could've flowed from them. My mind couldn't fathom what was happening, my mouth couldn't speak how I felt, and my body was confined under a blanket in a fetal position, trying to hide from the world around it. This is what broken feels like. This is what broken looks like. Are you currently in a season of brokenness? How do you find joy in a season like this? How do you get out of brokenness? How do you escape the weight of it all? The answer is God. Most often God takes us through a season of brokenness so that we can find him more deeply. Many times our purpose is attached directly to our brokenness. God transforms the most broken moments of our lives into something powerful that brings him glory. This is how "The Lost Butterflies" was developed. I turned my pain into purpose to ultimately bring God glory and help others heal their wounds by sharing our journey. Is it easy? No, not at all, but anything is possible with God. As you become more aware of the goodness of God despite your circumstances, you will see God more clearly in the midst of your storms. Never underestimate the power of God in any season of your life.

"When I am afraid, I put my trust in you."

Psalm 56:3

Are you currently in a season of brokenness?
In what ways can you heal?
How can you turn your pain into purpose?

The beauty of the journey is not in glorifying all of its ups, but instead finding meaning in all of its downs.

-Angelica Gunn

When God Says No

As I sit and look back on our journey, I realize that all of those years were filled with noes from God. There were many moments when we felt like we deserved a yes but instead repeatedly received a no. I often would become angry with God because we were good people and I felt we didn't deserve this level of pain. We desperately wanted another child, we prayed for another child, but sometimes what we want and our idea of timing isn't what God has planned for us. So many failed cycles, failed tests, failed pregnancies, and failed plans. But were they really failures, or were they all a part of God's plan to turn our pain into purpose, giving us a story to tell to share his glory with the world?

God's no isn't always just a no; sometimes it's a "not right now." Our layout of how our lives will go, our visions for how things will happen, may not always align with God's vision. We must understand *that* in order to truly be able to process the seasons in which God tells us no.

We must also include God in our plans and remind ourselves of the promises he's given to us so that in moments of weakness and defeat we don't get lost in the pain. We often get so stuck on the fact that God has told us no in a certain season of our lives that we miss all of the lessons tied to that no and all of the insight he is trying to give us to be used in the future. Be still and know what God's plan is for you. Though right now you may feel empty and defeated, God is not done with you, and his promises still remain. Change how you perceive your journey, change your perspective, and watch how God starts to move in and shift things in your life.

The hardest thing for me during our journey was trying to turn negative thoughts into positive thoughts. Let's face it, many of us struggle with this daily. Not only does it affect our relationships, it affects our overall health and well-being. We have to be honest with ourselves, and work harder at focusing on God and maintaining a positive mindset through difficult times.

I had become so used to disappointment that I allowed it to change my thought patterns from positive to negative. My mind would automatically think something bad before something good, and I knew that I needed to heal deep within myself in order to rid my mind of this pattern of thinking. Disappointment often will leave us feeling as if our lives have come crashing down and will rob us of our hope for better days. When the weight of failure continues to press down on us, my husband and I turn to God in prayer. It is the only answer to our fears, doubts, and defeat. Through prayer, we open our hearts up more to allowing God in, to hearing more from God, and to finding hope in the promises he whispers to us daily. Prayer is our greatest weapon. It is how we build a true relationship with God and how we communicate with God daily.

I want to include a brief paragraph from a letter I wrote to our first angel baby to give you an example of how I used a moment in which God told us no as a way to pray and acknowledge my hurt and the loss of our baby.

Dear Baby Bear,

I deeply wanted you. I screamed with joy the moment I knew you were in my womb. I had longed for you for so long, and I feel like all of that joy was ripped from my soul now that you are wrapped in God's arms. How did we get here? What did I do wrong? Why is this happening? Why would God allow us to go through all of the waiting and trials with secondary infertility, to now becoming pregnant, carrying you for 12 weeks, and then taking you away from us so swiftly? The pain of losing you left me physically, mentally, emotionally, and spiritually broken into a million pieces. I cried tears I never knew I had, I screamed in agony, my heart ached in grief, and my mind was completely withdrawn from the world around me. All I could think of was you, all I could feel was empty, all I could see was blood and a sac that embraced every part of you, still complete and intact. They tried to tell me you didn't exist. They tried to tell me the sac was empty, a "blighted ovum," they said, but I saw you with my own two eyes. I knew you were there all along, even though lifeless. I knew you existed. I knew you were real, but yet the scans and tests all showed nothing. You were hidden, lost in Mommy's womb, and though part of me knew you were there and deeply wanted you to stay, it wasn't enough to save you.

-Mommy

But when you pray, go into your room, close the door and pray to your Father, who is unseen. Then your Father, who sees what is done in secret, will reward you.

Matthew 6:6

And we know that in all things God works for the good of those who love him, who have been called according to his purpose.

Romans 8:28

"I wait for the Lord, my whole being waits, and in his word I put my hope."

Psalm 130:5

Can you still accept God's plan when it doesn't go the way you want? Can you still see God in the midst of failure?

Healing from Deep Wounds

This pain runs deep, so much so that I can feel it in my soul. After experiencing a miscarriage, the scars left behind are often damaging, heartbreaking, and unfathomable. When I think of the many wounds left behind after our miscarriages, I think about how as a kid I would fall down and scrape my knee. I think about how it would bleed and cause a lot of pain, and as the wound would begin to try to heal, it would form a scab over it. Many times the scab would fall off, the wound would get bumped and scraped again, and the healing process would have to start over. Healing from miscarriage is hard, and many times I have to start the healing process over, as emotions overcome me and the scars of my womb resurface. Most days I've found that my only true way of healing is to go to God in prayer, simply asking for his help, guidance, and love. "He heals the brokenhearted and binds up their wounds," Psalm 147:3. I tried finding healing on my own, but all I was left with was disappointment. Most often we try to find our healing in other people or by masking our wounds with overeating, alcohol consumption, depression, etc. None of these things can heal us. In fact, they tend to just make things worse and cause us to fall deeper into depression. You can't fight battles with things; the only way to fight is with the armor of God. So put down the ego, the negative thinking, the drinking, the overeating, and whatever else you may be masking your grief with, and invite God to step in and fight the battles for you.

I realized that relying on other people to get me through this season of my life was unfair to them. We tend to put our problems onto our families and friends, thinking that they should have all the answers. Then, when we don't receive the response or answers we are looking for, we become upset, revert back to our shell and hiding place, or become angry. The only true listener that we should be speaking our hearts fully to is God. When I began pouring my heart out to God, he began to pour his light and oil back into me, I found new purpose with his guidance, I found healing, I found love, and above all, I found PEACE.

I encourage you to PRAY over it,
PRAY for it,
and PRAY through it.

Prayer is our greatest weapon for any battle we may be facing.

Take this time now to begin to cry out to God in prayer, make your request known to God, and pray for healing and restoration of your heart.

"For no word from God will ever fail." Luke 1:37

"Lord my God, I called to you for help, and you healed me."
Psalm 30:2

How deep are your wounds? Are you still healing from past wounds? How has your miscarriage/pregnancy loss affected your ability to pray to God? What other barriers are preventing you from seeking God for true healing?

Do not let your faith waver in this season. The void and emptiness you feel can only be healed by God. Open your heart, change your posture, and allow God to move on your behalf.

-Angelica Gunn

Finding Peace after Loss

Losing our babies traumatized us. It left us with a void that can never be filled. Most days we are fine, but then grief will hit us like a ton of bricks and take the wind out of us. There is no road map to peace after loss. The only true provider of peace in seasons like this is God. A verse that I referred to often during our journey was John 14:27: "Peace I leave with you; my peace I give to you. I do not give to you as the world gives. Do not let your hearts be troubled and do not be afraid." Whenever I would read that verse, I would instantly feel relieved of the pressures of grief. What is peace? It is being and feeling free from war or disturbance. So much of my heart desired peace during this season of our lives. I wanted to be able to wake up feeling peaceful and not broken. Fighting for peace is a daily fight. It takes true courage and a warrior mindset to put on the whole armor of God each day and go to war with your thoughts, your battles, your scars, and your brokenness. I spent most of my days just trying to turn my negative thinking into positive thinking, and that is still a struggle some days.

Peace helps us accomplish our life's purpose. When we are fully at peace, life flows more freely and our energy isn't disrupted when trials come. Peace gives us the ability to refrain from allowing the enemy to have control over us. When we are at peace, we are in a true place of healing and restoration. I want you to just take a few seconds to get in tune with your thoughts and your breathing, and once you are comfortable with where you are and feel a sense of calmness, I want you to take three deep breaths, inhale/exhale, and release all negative thoughts. As you release these thoughts, replace them with positive alternatives, and watch how quickly that starts to help release some weight off of you. Did that help release some tension? Do you feel a slight relief? Were you able to replace your negative thoughts with positive thoughts? Meditation is a great way to recenter yourself and to become in tune with your thought patterns. I find that morning meditation truly sets the tone for my day and helps me to focus and have a better attitude throughout my day. Do what's best for you: if meditation isn't your thing, then try music or writing in a journal before you start your day and set the tone for how peace will show up in your life.

"Now may the Lord of peace himself give you peace at all times and in every way. The Lord be with all of you."

2 Thessalonians 3:16

What brings you peace? What has helped calm your spirit during this season of loss?

Hoping for a Rainbow

During our journey through secondary infertility and recurrent miscarriages, we created a "Hope" box. In this box we placed baby items with hopes of one day actually getting to use them. We also placed letters to our babies in it, as well as all of our pregnancy tests that ended in miscarriage, believing that one day a positive test would lead to a successful full-term pregnancy. We bought onesies here and there, baby books, a rainbow baby outfit, baby moccasins, and stuffed animals. Whenever we would feel weak, doubtful, and defeated during our journey, we would go back to this box for hope and light. The hardest thing to do during seasons of grief is remain hopeful. I encourage you to do something to keep your hope alive and bring joy to you during moments when you're completely overwhelmed. Many times tears were falling down my face as I sat before this box. I would hold the stuffed animals and cry my eyes out, but afterwards, I would feel better. In this box we also kept a prayer to remind us to go to God in prayer with our needs and release our burdens to God so that we might be relieved of the weight bearing down on us.

Dear God,

We come before you, asking that you relieve us of the pain, emptiness, and brokenness of our miscarriages. We ask that you heal our hearts and our minds as we try to move forward without our babies in our arms. We ask for peace, trusting that you have us in your arms and have full control. We ask that you help us to remain hopeful in this season, to not allow our present pain to kill our dreams and desires of having another child. We ask you for strength to get us through the difficult days ahead of us and help us to always hold our babies in our hearts. Amen.

Your prayer may be different, but it is imperative that you pray from your heart, that you speak life and not death over your journey. Prayer changes things, and the more you pray, the more in tune you become with God's plan for your life and your situation. Cast all your cares on him and have hope that one day everything you've placed in your hope box will be used. Though our hope box had to be continuously filled and prayed over for three years, all of our HOPE turned into pure JOY when our rainbow baby, our son Caleb, was born. God gave us Caleb when we needed him most. He is our rainbow after the storm, he is the light of our lives, his personality lights up every room he encounters, he is truly heaven-sent.

"I consider that our present sufferings are not worth comparing with the glory that will be revealed in us."

Romans 8:18

Do you find joy in dreaming of your rainbow? Do you find hope in knowing that one day the rain will stop, the sun will shine, and a rainbow will appear?

Turning Pain into Purpose

Our pain is purposeful: it is the true essence of who we become as individuals. Our pain tells so many stories that so many others can relate to. God will use what we see as seasons of pain and heartache as means to provide healing and deliverance to others. Someone's deliverance is tied to my obedience, I truly believe that. Is it easy to share? No, not at all, but sharing our journey is not about me or my husband. It is about giving glory to God for bringing us through one of the darkest seasons in our lives and helping others get through their seasons. I battled with the decision to share and speak out for years. I knew God wanted me to, but I was hesitant due to not being completely healed and being shy and afraid of what others would think. I needed to process our journey and heal, but God continuously pursued me, spoke to me, and asked me to move, so I began to listen and open my heart more to doing his will for my life. No matter where you are in your journey, someone can be touched by it, someone can relate to it, and someone needs to hear it to know that they are not alone. The more I started to share, the more people started to respond and share their stories with me.

It made me realize that our journey and our pain was never about us. God will break you to position you and mold you into purpose. He uses our pain to produce fruit in our dry seasons. All of our tears, our heartache, our losses brought us closer to God, allowed God to use our journey for his glory, and provided us with a beautiful testimony to share with the world. Be still and know that he is God. Trust in him and his plans for you. Free yourself of every burden, for he cares for you. Stop worrying and trying to figure it all out on your own, and allow God to be God in your life.

My whole life I had been giving more than I would ever receive in return. I continuously gave more of myself away than I had to give. I realized how much giving cost me. It cost me my peace, my sanity, my self-love, my worth, my heart, and my babies. Giving to others literally sucked the life out of me, and it wasn't until now that I realized the lessons God had hidden in the midst of our storms. We wanted another baby so bad that we obsessed over it, and God used it as a season to teach us a lesson. God said, "I'll give you what you asked for but not in the manner of which you asked for it.

Because if I give it to you just how you asked, what will you do? Obsess over it, and forget about me?" We experienced three losses, but I didn't realize what God was doing until now. We wanted another baby so bad that it cost us. He didn't give us babies, he gave us angels instead.When I began to change my perspective, God gave me understanding that even in all of our pain he still blessed us with three angels to continuously watch over us, guide us, and be with us always. In that moment, I felt God's grace. I know its hard, I know it hurts, and I know it's easy to just be angry and upset. We must release all of what we are feeling in this moment, and allow God to provide us with strength to keep fighting through our tough seasons. Many nights, I would just kneel before God and my tears would begin to flow uncontrollably. I didn't have any words to offer God in those moments, but my tears where communicating to God for me. Sometimes it's okay to just kneel before God, even if you have nothing to say in those moments, just allow God to see your posture and feel your need for guidance and love. Nothing is too big for God, so put your trust in him.

"My grace is sufficient for you, for my power is made perfect in weakness."

2 Corinthians 12:9

Do you feel that your pain can be tied into your purpose? What have you developed within yourself in this season?

Holding on to God's Promises

Beautiful, despite where you are, despite how you feel, despite your circumstances, God is still good, he is still faithful, and his promises to you still remain. I know how hard it is to wake up and believe that each day, especially when you are going through such a difficult season, but God's love for you hasn't changed. He knows your paths before you ever encounter them, he sees you, he's listening, and he's waiting for you to trust him again. He sees you hurting, he sees your tears, but this is not the end for you. God is going to allow something new to be born in you and through you despite your current situation. God's word will never return to him void. He is a promise keeper, and what he says is true. It's easy to lose sight of God and his promises during seasons of trauma, grief, loss, and disappointment, but even through all of that, God still never leaves your side. Hold on to the hope that God has a plan for you and that he has not forgotten about you.

"God is our refuge and strength, an ever-present help in trouble."
Psalm 46:1

Will you stay true to God's promise? How will you apply God's word to your journey? What will you do when your promise doesn't come when you expect it to? Don't give up. God's promises to you still remain. No matter what this season looks like, he is still God, and miracles can happen.

Undeniable Expectations

Expectation is the belief that something you hope for is certain to happen. Lack of trust in God affects our ability to expect greater things from him. Our prior disappointments cause us to limit God and all he can do. God can do the unimaginable. Nothing is impossible for God. Our expectations of God are undeniable to him. He desires to give us all that he has for us despite how our circumstances make us feel. What expectations and desires have you let go of because of your past denials and disappointments? What is blocking you from truly trusting in God and his promises to you? Many times throughout our journey, my husband and I became accustomed to everything going wrong, and our expectation that something could go right was very minimal. We had lots of doubt in the beginning due to all of the scars and hurt inside of us. It took lots of prayer, tears, and understanding for us to truly see that God is still good no matter what our seasons look like. He is still faithful and can still do the unimaginable. In order to truly walk in an undeniable expectational mindset, we must truly trust God at his word.

"But now, Lord, what do I look for? My hope is in you." Psalm 39:7

Have you felt let down due to the expectations you've place on God, or yourself? How can you change your perspective? In what ways can you release your expectations and trust God at his word?

Thank You

Thank you for purchasing, reading, and participating in this journal. I pray that you gained something from it and that it will help you on your journey to healing. Remember, take your time, breathe, and allow yourself to feel and know that you are not alone. I want to end this book with a special prayer for you.

Dear God,

I pray for the woman reading this prayer journal. Though I may not be aware of her story, I am aware of her needs. I pray for her broken heart and the emptiness she feels in her soul. I ask that you meet her right where she is right now and begin to wrap your arms around her and move on her behalf. I pray that you heal her womb, her heart, and her mind. I pray for peace over her life and that you would remind her of how beautiful and wonderfully made she is. Be with her in her moments of sadness, comfort her during times of loneliness, and love her through all of her pain. Amen.

Acknowledgments

Thank you to the many warrior women I have encountered on this journey. Thank you for uplifting and inspiring me to share our story. Thank you to my husband, Caleb, for the constant encouragement, support, and love throughout writing this book. Many days I felt defeated in my efforts, but he never allowed me to give up. Thank you to our children, Ai'Kayla and CJ, for the constant love and understanding when Mommy needed quiet time to write. Thank you to all of our friends and family for their support and encouragement throughout writing this book. I greatly appreciate you all and truly hope this book touches you in some way.

Contact Info

Follow me on Instagram

@thelostbutterflies.

For donations, send to

paypal.me/thelostbutterflies.

For booking/speaking engagements contact

me via email:

thelostbutterfliesfoundation@gmail.com.

CPSIA information can be obtained
at www.ICGtesting.com
Printed in the USA
LVHW020846111122
732762LV00013B/687

9 780578 960838